BY GEORGE, BLOOMERS!

Shoe Tree Press

BY GEORGE, BLOOMERS!

BY JUDITH ST. GEORGE

illustrated by Margot Tomes

Published by Shoe Tree Press
an imprint of Betterway Publications, Inc.
P.O. Box 219, Crozet, VA 22932, (804) 823-5661

Text ● 1976, 1989 by Judith St. George
Illustrations ● 1976, 1989 by Margot Tomes

Originally published in 1976 by
Coward, McCann & Geoghegan, Inc.

Library of Congress Cataloging-in-Publication Data

St. George, Judith
    By George, Bloomers!/by Judith St. George :
illustrated by Margot Tomes.
    p. cm.
    Summary: Eight-year-old Hannah meets with
her mother's disapproval when she wants to wear
the new women's garment, bloomers, which cause
a mild sensation when they are introduced in the
mid-nineteenth century.
    ISBN 1-55870-135-4: : $5.95
    [1. Women's rights--Fiction. 2. Sex role--
Fiction.]   I. Tomes, Margot, ill.   II. Title.
PZ7.S142By   1989
[Fic]--dc20
                                    89-17898
                                        CIP
                                         AC

Printed in the United States of America
0 9 8 7 6 5 4 3 2 1

For Sarah
and her friend Amy

CONTENTS

Chapter One
TAD AND JOEL SING A SONG

Hannah and Tad and Joel
sat on a fence eating cherries.
They were having a contest.
Who could spit cherry pits the farthest?

Hannah was winning.
Suddenly Tad jumped off the fence.
"Quick, hide," he whispered.
"Here comes Mrs. Bloomer.
And she's wearing
those baggy pants."
Tad and Joel hid behind the fence.
They pulled Hannah down beside them.

Mrs. Bloomer walked past.

Hi Ho,
In sleet and snow,
Mrs. Bloomer's all the go.
Twenty tailors to take the stitches,
Plenty of women to wear the britches.

Tad and Joel chanted.

Mrs. Bloomer looked over the fence.
"Good morning, boys.
And isn't that Hannah Willis?
Good morning, Hannah,"
she said with a smile.
Mrs. Bloomer was one of the first ladies
to wear pants in the whole United States.
Bloomers were named after her.

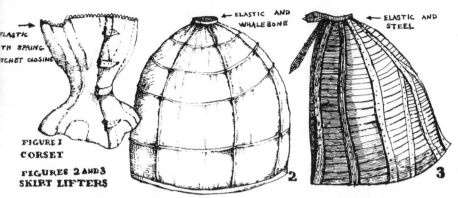

ELASTIC AND
WHALEBONE

ELASTIC AND
STEEL

ELASTIC
TH SPRING
TCHET CLOSING

FIGURE I
CORSET

FIGURES 2 AND 3
SKIRT LIFTERS

2

3

Most ladies wore tight corsets and petticoats
with long, full skirts that dragged in the mud.

THE LILY.

IN INTERESTS OF WOMAN

AMELIA BLOOMER

EDITOR AND PUBLISHER

SENECA FALLS, N.Y. AUG., 1852

Mrs. Bloomer owned a newspaper, too.
She wrote stories about how comfortable
long pants were to wear.
She wanted all women to try them.

Hannah didn't like Tad and Joel's song.
She wanted to wear bloomers herself.
If she wore bloomers
she could skate
like the wind on the canal.
Or walk on stilts.
Or be the first up the tree house
instead of the last.

But Mama would never
let Hannah wear bloomers.
Mama always wore a bonnet and gloves
and carried a parasol.
Mama said, "Bloomers are *disgraceful*.
Women who wear them, like Mrs. Bloomer,
have crazy ideas.
Why, some women even want
to have the vote.
A real lady isn't interested
in such things.
Always act like a lady,"
Mama told Hannah.
But Hannah had never
seen a lady
ride on a rope swing
or play snap-the-whip.
Hannah was only eight.
She didn't care
about being a lady at all.

Chapter Two
A TALK WITH MAMA AND PAPA

When Hannah got home
with her pail of cherries,
Mama and Papa were arguing.
Hannah knew they were arguing
because Mama didn't say anything
about her dirty dress
and torn stockings.
And Papa said,
"Well, well, here's Hannah,"
as if he were surprised to see her.
They were arguing
about Papa's sister, Lucy.
Aunt Lucy was coming for a visit.
"Whatever will I do with
Lucy for a whole week?" Mama said.
"She's so . . . so . . . different."
Papa could see that Hannah was listening.
"I know you and Lucy
will have fun," he said.
"I'm sure they will," Mama said.
"Lucy can spend the week
playing hopscotch with Hannah

and flying kites with Jamie."
Papa laughed. Hannah laughed, too.
She looked forward to Aunt Lucy's visit.

17

Chapter Three
THE YELLOW KITE

Aunt Lucy was arriving by train.
The whole family planned to meet her.
Hannah and her brother Jamie were
so excited that they were ready early.
Hannah wore her Scotch plaid dress,
three petticoats, stockings, lace pantalets,
a bonnet, and gloves.
Jamie wore his sailor suit.

They waited on the front porch
for Mama and Papa.
Jamie held a new yellow kite.
He was only four and too small to fly it.
"Can you get my kite in the air?"
he asked Hannah.
Hannah ran with the kite.
It bumped along the ground.

She heard a laugh behind her.
"Ha, ha. A girl flying a kite.
That beats all."
It was Tad!
He and Joel were watching
from Tad's tree house next door.
Hannah was angry.
She held the kite with one hand
and her skirt with the other.

She ran faster and faster.
Hannah forgot about
her mother's flower garden.
There was a fence around it
to keep out rabbits.
Hannah's skirt caught on the fence.
She fell and landed on the flowers.
They broke under her.

Chapter Four
AUNT LUCY

When the train stopped,
Papa saw Aunt Lucy first.
She had a round pink face
and bouncing curls.
And she was wearing bloomers!
"Oh, Lucy, you look wonderful," Papa said.
He smiled and gave Lucy a big kiss.

"Oh, Lucy, what will everyone
say?" Mama asked.
"They will say I have good sense,"
Aunt Lucy answered.
"By George, this is 1852.
Women are standing up for their rights,
and wearing bloomers is one way to do it.
No woman can be free
to work, to study, to teach,
if she's tripping over big full skirts."

Hannah watched Aunt Lucy jump
into the buggy.
She held a parrot cage in one hand
and a carpetbag in the other.
She had no skirts to hold onto at all.
"Oh, Mama, I would like to
wear bloomers, too," Hannah said.
"Humph," Mama replied.
Hannah knew
her mother's "humph" meant no.
Jamie thought Aunt Lucy's bloomers
looked funny, too.
For a while

he even forgot his kite.
But when they got home
he pointed to the roof.
"My kite," he howled.
"By George, your kite looks

very handsome up there," Aunt Lucy said.
"But I want to fly it," Jamie complained.
"I'll fetch it later
when I get home from work,"
Papa said.
And he drove off in his buggy.

After Papa left,
Aunt Lucy played with Jamie.
First she pulled him in his wagon.
Then she pushed him in the swing.
When Jamie went upstairs for his nap
Aunt Lucy rolled hoops with Hannah.
Hannah was good.
But Aunt Lucy was better.
In her bloomers, Aunt Lucy

28

ran faster than Hannah
and whacked the hoop harder.
Hannah tried to keep up with her.
Swish.
Hannah's hoop hit a rock,
flew over the fence,
and rolled in the street.
Aunt Lucy ran to catch it.
But she didn't open the gate
like most people.
She jumped right over the fence.

There was laughter from next door.
Tad and Joel were still in their tree house.
They were laughing at Aunt Lucy!

Hi Ho,
In sleet and snow,
Mrs. Bloomer's all the go.
Twenty tailors to take the stitches,
Plenty of women to wear the britches.

they sang out.
Hannah was furious.

She marched over to the tree house.
"Don't you dare tease my Aunt Lucy,"
she shouted. "You're horrid and mean,
and you're not my friends."
The boys poked their heads
out the tree house window
and laughed even harder.

Hannah climbed the tree house ladder.
She was almost at the top
when her dress caught on a nail.
Her skirt ripped all the way up the front.
The boys hooted and whistled.
Mama leaned out the kitchen window.

"Hannah, can't you ever act like a lady?
Look at your dress. Ruined.
Go to your room this minute."
Mama closed the kitchen window
with a bang.

Hannah thumped all the way upstairs
to her room.
Who wanted to act like a lady?
She stared in the looking glass.
Her skirt looked *almost* like bloomers.
Hadn't Mama said her dress was ruined?

Hannah took off her pantalets
and her three petticoats.
Then she ripped the skirt down the back
and tied the torn pieces around her ankles.
There! *Now* they were bloomers.
Hannah heard a knock at the door.
"Come in," she called.
Aunt Lucy opened the door and peeked in.
She smiled when she saw
Hannah's bloomers.
"Now we both have
good sense," she said.
She helped Hannah tie the legs tighter.
Hannah turned around and around
in front of the looking glass.
She was so pleased with her bloomers,
she made a silly face.
"When we roll hoops—"
Hannah started to say.
She was cut off by a frightened cry.
"Mama, help!"
It sounded like Jamie.

Chapter Five
A CRY FOR HELP

Hannah and Aunt Lucy ran from the room.
They met Mama hurrying up the stairs.
"MAMA!"
It *was* Jamie.
He was somewhere above them.
They headed for the attic stairs.
Mama had to hold up her skirts.
She ran the slowest

and was the last to reach the attic.
Hannah and Aunt Lucy and Mama
ran from room to room.
There was no Jamie.
"He sounded far away," Mama said.
"As if he were outside," Aunt Lucy added.
Hannah remembered the long closet
where she and Jamie played dress-up.
There was a tiny window at the end of it.
Hannah pushed open the closet door.
The closet was empty,
but the window was open.

Mama and Aunt Lucy
and Hannah ran to the window.
They looked out.
Jamie was on the roof with his new yellow kite.
"Jamie, don't move," Mama gasped.
She was very pale.

Aunt Lucy tried to squeeze through the window.

Then Mama tried.
They were much too big
and the window was much too small.

"I can fit," Hannah said.
And in her trim bloomers, she could.
"We'll tie a rope around you
so you won't fall," Aunt Lucy said.
Mama found a rope.
Aunt Lucy tied it around Hannah's waist.
She tied the other end to a big trunk.
Hannah swung her legs over
the high windowsill
and climbed out.
In her bloomers it was easy.
"Stay with Jamie until help comes,"
Aunt Lucy called.

Hannah was very high up.
She looked down on the tree house.
She saw Jamie's wagon on the lawn.
It looked as small as a toy.
Jamie was crying.
"I came out to get my kite,
but now I'm scared," he sobbed.
Hannah sat down beside Jamie and
held him tight.
"Let's go in," Jamie begged.
"Please."
Hannah looked back up at the attic window.
She was scared, too.
But she was sure she could make it.
"All right," she said.
She lowered Jamie's kite
down to the ground.
And they started out.
Though the roof was very steep,
she was as surefooted as Tad or Joel.
And without a skirt
and petticoats to hold,
her hands were free to help
Jamie the whole way.

When they reached the window,
Mama pulled Jamie through.
She hugged him tightly.
Hannah followed Jamie into the attic.
Mama hugged her tightly, too.
Aunt Lucy had gone for help.
But no help was needed.
Hannah had saved Jamie all by herself.

Chapter Six
HANNAH'S SURPRISE

On the day Aunt Lucy was to leave,
Hannah and her mother stayed upstairs
until Papa and Jamie and Aunt Lucy
were seated in the buggy.
"We're waiting for you," Papa called.
"Just a minute," Mama answered.
She and Hannah came

45

out of the house together.
Mama was wearing a pink flowered dress.
Hannah was wearing green bloomers.
Papa and Jamie and Aunt Lucy
laughed and clapped.
"Could that young lady be wearing bloomers?"
Papa teased.
"By George, they *look* like bloomers,"
Aunt Lucy said.
Mama put her arm around Hannah.

"They *feel* like bloomers," Mama agreed.
Hannah skipped down the front walk.
She turned a cartwheel,
then jumped into the buggy.
"They *act* like bloomers, too."

AUTHOR'S NOTE

Hannah, Mama, Papa, Jamie, and Aunt Lucy are a make-believe family. But Mrs. Amelia Bloomer was a real person. She lived in Seneca Falls, New York, where the first Woman's Rights Convention was held in 1848. Mrs. Bloomer published her own newspaper. She was also one of the first women to wear long pants. Because Mrs. Bloomer told everyone how comfortable long pants were, other women began to wear them, too. Soon the long pants were called "the bloomer costume" or "bloomers."

During Mrs. Bloomer's time, women started talking about improving their lives. Women wanted to vote. They wanted to be treated fairly by the law. They wanted a good education. They wanted to hold good jobs, just like men. In 1848 they weren't able to do any of these things. In the 1850's women got together to talk about changing the laws. Some of these ladies wore bloomers.

Most people, like Mama and Tad and Joel, thought bloomers looked funny. They laughed at the women who wore them. Sometimes children chanted the same song that Tad and Joel sang to Mrs. Bloomer and Aunt Lucy. The women didn't mind the teasing. But people laughed at their new ideas, too. And the women *did* mind that. Winning new rights was very important to them and they wanted people to take their ideas seriously. When their bloomers made people laugh at what they were trying to do, after two or three years, women stopped wearing them.

Nowadays, women wear pants whenever they want to. A lady is no longer judged by whether she wears pants or skirts. But some people still don't take women seriously when they speak out for their rights and what they believe in. So the women's movement for full equality continues.